When his room was a mess,
Eric liked it best.

"It's your room. Keep it the way you like it," his mom said as she played croquet down the hallway.

"Your room is a jungle! I'm sure there are strange plants growing in there somewhere," his dad said as he dunked a basketball into the bathroom sink.

"Eeeeeeee!" his baby sister Sally squealed as she finger-painted the walls.

One day, his mom roller-skated around the corner and peeked inside Eric's room with a special interest.

"Does your room have a floor?" she asked.

Eric stood on his head and pointed his toes toward the ceiling.

"When you're upside down, you can see a floor," he said.

"Yes. Perfect for dancing," his mom agreed.
She strapped on her ballet shoes and leapt inside.

She was lost all morning. Eventually, Eric found her tangled up in his race track. She was playing marbles with the dice from a board game.

Eric helped her out of his room.

"NONSENSE! NO ONE IS LOST IN A ROOM," HIS DAD SAID.
HE LOOKED IN ERIC'S ROOM . . . AND TURNED PALE.
HIS KNEES SHOOK.

But he was a brave man.
He put on his fencing outfit and lunged inside.

They waited and waited.
Finally, they started dinner without him.
But Eric could not eat until he found his dad.

Stuck between a huge stuffed dinosaur and a gumball machine, his dad was counting the stuffed animals around him.

Eric helped him out of the room.

After that, Eric made his parents kiss him good night at his door.

He tucked himself into bed.

Eric's baby sister Sally crawled inside and was lost for a whole day.

Eric's grandparents strapped backpacks on and started inside to find her.

Eric stopped them.

"Wait here," Eric said.

When Eric helped out his baby sister Sally, she wanted to crawl back inside.

She wanted to spend more time eating the crackers that had mysteriously vanished from the kitchen cupboard the day before.

Eric built a Wall and Many Fences in Front of his door so his baby Sister Sally Would Not crawl inside again.

Strange sounds came from inside Eric's room.

His friends and relatives tiptoed carefully past.

Once, a vacuum salesman came by.
"I can handle anything," the salesman said.

THey
Let
HiM
parachute
iNSide.

He was lost for a week.

Eric finally found him tucked up inside an old map of the universe.

When Eric helped him out, he had lost his vacuum.

"You can keep it!" the salesman shouted as he ran away.

The mess crept up and up until it spilt over the wall and fences and into the hallway. It moved on and on through the house.

Eric helped his family escape through a window.

"No. I would have to spend a year finding them all," Eric said. "I will clean my room now."

"You are so brave," his mom said. She hugged him.

"Good luck," his dad said.

He gave a four-leaf clover to Eric.

Eric disappeared inside.

When he had finished, Eric invited his family into his room.

They could not believe it!

They stared and stared.

"Your room is tidy. We can tuck you in at night again," his mom said.

"And we can kiss you good night afterwards," his dad said.

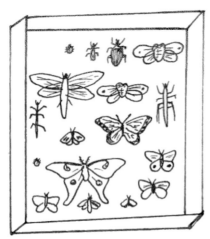

The next day, Eric's baby sister Sally crawled inside his room again.

This time, she wasn't lost.

This time, she sat down and cried.

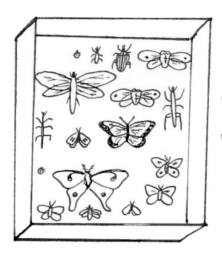

"Don't cry," Eric said as he patted her. "My room will get messy again."

To mess-makers everywhere, especially the ones in our families.
JH & JM

Made in the USA
San Bernardino, CA
16 September 2019